BY **ELISE PETERSEN**
ILLUSTRATED BY **IZA TRAPANI**

Whispering Coyote Press
Dallas

TRACY'S MESS

To Tracy
Love, Mom
−E.P.

For Kelly, who inspired these paintings.
With Love

−I.T.

Published by Whispering Coyote Press
300 Crescent Court, Suite 860
Dallas, TX 75201
Text copyright © 1996 by Elise Petersen
Illustrations copyright © 1996 by Iza Trapani
All rights reserved including the right of reproduction
in whole or in part in any form.

Printed in Hong Kong by South China Printing Company (1988) Ltd.
Book production and design by THE KIDS AT OUR HOUSE
10 9 8 7 6 5 4 3 2 1

Library of Congress Cataloging-in-Publication Data

Petersen, Elise, 1960-
Tracy's mess / written by Elise Petersen ; illustrated by Iza Trapani.
p.   cm.
Summary: Messy Tracy faces a dilemma when her mother tells her to clean her room.
ISBN 1-58089-003-2(paperback) : $5.95
[1. Cleanliness−Fiction. 2. Orderliness−Fiction.] I. Trapani, Iza, ill. II. Title.
PZ7.P44335Tr 1996
[E]−dc2−   95-30690
                        CIP
                        AC

Tracy Petersen is, I bet,
the messiest girl I've ever met.
Six years old and four feet tall,
you'd never guess she was messy at all.
With every little curl in place,
a gentle smile upon her face.

But here's a warning—take a broom
if you ever go inside her room.

Toys are thrown across the floor,
dolls and hats behind the door.

A jelly sandwich is on her bed.
I don't know where she lays her head.
Her favorite kitty is upside down.
It used to be pink, but now it's brown.

Sweaters, crayons, books, and balls,
cars, and puppets, paper dolls,
pictures, papers, dogs, and blocks,
teddy bears, and dirty socks,
pencils, boxes, bows, and lace,
not one thing was put in place.

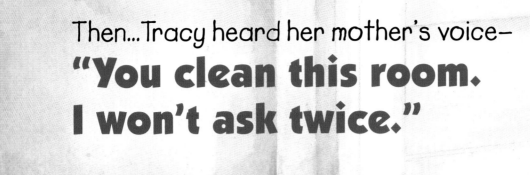

Then...Tracy heard her mother's voice—
"You clean this room. I won't ask twice."

But Tracy had a plan instead—
she would hide her toys beneath her bed.
Her jelly sandwich and her blocks,
the teddy bears and dirty socks,

the sweaters, crayons, books, and balls,
cars, and puppets, paper dolls,
the papers, pencils, and bows of red.
All were stuffed beneath her bed.

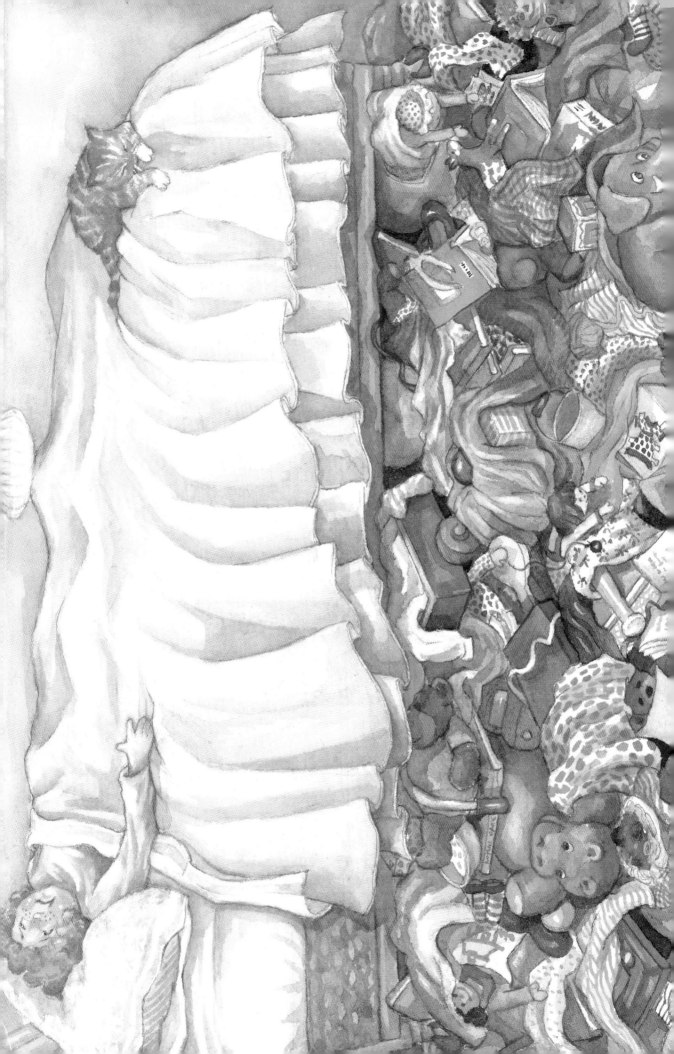

Then Tracy gave a heavy sigh,
because her bed was very high.
And when she went to bed that night
her blankets touched the ceiling light...

So in the morning Tracy said,
"I'd better clean beneath my bed."
She put away the crayon box,
the paper dolls and dirty socks,

the jelly sandwich and the bows,
(how she did it, no one knows).
The blocks, and sweaters, books, and ball.
Somehow Tracy cleaned it all.

So now her bedroom has a floor...
but just don't open the closet door!